Dark Man

Escape from the Dark

by Peter Lancett

illustrated by Jan Pedroietta

D1076817

Dark Man

Escape from the Dark
by Peter Lancett
illustrated by Jan Pedroietta

Published by Ransom Publishing Ltd.
Rose Cottage, Howe Hill, Watlington, Oxon. OX49 5HB
www.ransom.co.uk

ISBN 184167 416 8

First published in 2005

Copyright © 2005 Ransom Publishing Ltd.

Chapter One:
The Girl

It is night.

The room is dark. The room is dirty.

The windows are broken.

The room is quiet.

A man sits on the floor.

His back rests against a wall.

The man looks up.

He hears the wooden stairs creak.

The door opens.

A girl stands in the door frame.

She sees the man and is afraid.

"Come in," he says.

The girl does not move.

Chapter Two:
The Touch

"Do not be afraid," the man says.

The girl takes one step into the room.

"Is it you?" the girl asks.

Her voice is shaky. She finds it hard to breathe.

"It is," the man says.

Slowly the girl walks over to him.

The man sees that she walks with a limp.

The girl holds out her hand.

In her hand is a note.

He takes the note.

His fingers touch the girl's fingers.

Inside his head there is a flash of light.

In a moment he sees the girl's illness.

He sees why she walks with a limp.

He sees why she finds it hard to breathe.

The girl is very ill.

Chapter Three:
The Escape

Dark Man reads the note.

"There is more," the girl says.

"On the way here to you, there were men. I think they were following me."

He stands. He brushes the dust from his coat.

"Yet still you came," he says. "That was very brave."

"The man who gave me the note said that it was important."

They hear the noise of a door opening.

Dark Man takes the girl's hands.

She feels warm where he touches her.

"Come," he says. "We must get out."

They hear footsteps on the stairs.

The room has a back door. He leads the
girl out of the back door.

They move fast but they make no sound.

Chapter Four:
The Girl Alone

They step out into the dark.

The night is cold.

"That was close," he says. "You must go now."

Soon the girl cannot see him.

He is lost in the shadows.

Then she notices …

She does not feel ill.

She can breathe, and it is easy to breathe.

She begins to walk, and now she can walk fast.

She no longer has a limp.

The End . . .

. . . for now . . .